A WIS ONE GOOD DEED

Written and Illustrated by
Adrienne Noel

For more information or to purchase
additional books visit my page:

www.adrienne-noel.com

Printed by Dynamic Marketing
18800 Beech Daly
Redford, MI 48420
www.dynamicmarketingllc.com

ISBN 978-0-9961158-1-0

A COLORFUL KITE FLIES THROUGH THE AIR,
AT THE END OF ITS STRING, A SQUIRREL FILLED WITH CARE.

THE SQUIRREL LOOKS UP TO THE SKY WITH ONLY ONE WISH,
THAT ALL LIVING THINGS COULD LIVE LIFE LESS SELFISH.

A DEER IS HUNGRY, WE LOOK THE OTHER WAY,
A DOG HAS NO HOME, HE HAS NO PLACE TO STAY.

LITTLE OWLS GROW UP WITHOUT BOOKS AND TOYS,
SO MUCH SADNESS FOR THOSE GIRLS AND BOYS.

A KITTEN SITS SHIVERING WITHOUT A COAT,
AND A SEA LION STRUGGLES TO STAY AFLOAT.

A LAMB WANDERS AROUND, OBVIOUSLY LOST, SHE CAN'T REMEMBER
WHERE SHE LIVES OR WHAT STREET SHE CROSSED.

A BIRD IS PERCHED ON A LIMB HIGH ABOVE,
WATCHING A LONELY SWAN WHO HAS LOST HIS TRUE LOVE.

TOO OFTEN WE IGNORE EACH OTHER WITH A SHRUG,
WHEN SOMETIMES IT COULD TAKE JUST ONE SIMPLE HUG.

WE NEED TO OPEN OUR EYES TO SEE THE LIGHT,
AND OPEN UP OUR HEARTS TO MAKE IT RIGHT.

IT ONLY TAKES ONE SIMPLE DEED,
TO HELP SOMEONE IN DESPERATE NEED.

THE SQUIRREL DIGS UP A NUT AND OFFERS IT TO THE DEER,
THE DEER SAYS, "THANKS BUT I CAN'T REPAY YOU, I FEAR."

THE SQUIRREL REPLIES, "ALL I ASK IS THAT YOU PASS ON THE FAVOR, I MADE YOU SMILE TODAY AND THAT I WILL SAVOR."

"IF EVERYONE DID ONE GOOD DEED A DAY,
AND TOLD THAT SOMEONE HOW TO REPAY..."

"WE ALL COULD LIVE IN A WORLD AS FREE AS MY KITE,
WARMING OUR SOULS AND MAKING OUR FUTURE SO BRIGHT."

THE DOG FINDS TOYS THAT WERE BEING THROWN OUT,
HE BRINGS THEM TO THE OWLS AND WATCHES THEM PLAY ABOUT.

THE OWLS' FATHER COMES OUT TO THANK THE LITTLE DOG,
AND BUILDS HIM A DOGHOUSE FROM A NEARBY LOG.

THE DEER RUSHES OVER TO HELP THE STRUGGLING SEAL,
"YOU SAVED MY LIFE, PLEASE STAY FOR A HOMEMADE MEAL."

THE LAMB SEES THE SHIVERING KITTEN AND PULLS OUT HER SHEARS,
SHE STARTS TO CUT AWAY HER WOOL, BEING CAREFUL BEHIND THE EARS.

THE KITTEN GUIDES THE LITTLE LAMB BACK TO HER HOME,
AND HEADS OVER TO THE POND WHERE THE BUFFALO ROAM.

A MONKEY ASKS THE BUFFALO TO TAKE HIM TO THE SWAN, "I'VE COME HERE TO OFFER FRIENDSHIP AND A SHOULDER TO CRY ON."

A BIRD APPROACHES THE SQUIRREL FLYING HIS KITE, AND TELLS THE STORY OF HIS BROKEN WING AND HOW HE COULDN'T TAKE FLIGHT.

HE EXPLAINS HOW A KIND RACCOON CAME TO HIS AID, AND SAID
"SOMEONE DID ME A FAVOR THAT NEEDS TO BE REPAID."

THE SQUIRREL SITS IN SHOCK THAT HIS WISH HAS COME TRUE,
"ONE GOOD DEED A DAY IS ALL YOU NEED TO DO!"